A-MUSING

Parable fairy-tales for kids and grown-ups

Lyudmila Kiseleva

Balboa Press books may be ordered through booksellers or by contacting:

Balboa Press
A Division of Hay House
1663 Liberty Drive
Bloomington, IN 47403
www.balboapress.com
1 (877) 407-4847

Because of the dynamic nature of the Internet, any web addresses or links contained in this book may have changed since publication and may no longer be valid. The views expressed in this work are solely those of the author and do not necessarily reflect the views of the publisher, and the publisher hereby disclaims any responsibility for them.

Any people depicted in stock imagery provided by Getty Images are models, and such images are being used for illustrative purposes only.
Certain stock imagery © Getty Images.

ISBN: 978-1-9822-1022-9 (sc)
ISBN: 978-1-9822-1023-6 (e)

Library of Congress Control Number: 2018909615

Print information available on the last page.

Balboa Press rev. date: 08/17/2018

BALBOA
PRESS
A DIVISION OF HAY HOUSE

A foreword for grown-ups

(not fairy-tale-ish)

You should talk, and talk, and talk to your children.

A foreword for children

(fairy-tale-ish)

Once upon a time there lived a *book*. No, actually it hasn't always lived, hasn't always existed. First the *book* was made up, written and an artist painted some nice pictures for it. And the book was just about to be published when the author realized the *book* had no name!

— What would you call me? — the book asked its author.

The author thought hard.

— It's not so easy, to come up with a name for you, *because a name should tell who you are written for and what you will live for...*

— Oh, that's easy, I know that, — the book said joyfully. — I am meant to be read. But who would want me: children or grown-ups?

— You are lucky for you are a very special book; you are for grown-ups and children at the same time. And your role, the purpose of your life is not only to be read. You will help grown-ups and children to talk to each other.

— And how will that happen?

— Oh, just like this: a mother will take you and read your tale to her Kid. The tale will be short, but everyone will understand that there is some meaning, hidden in it, and this meaning is to be discovered. What is locked in that simple story?

— Let's try musing over it, — Mom will tell her Kid. — It's amusing.

— So, what shall we do with my name? It hasn't been made up yet, has it?

— Why, it has, just now. You are called "A-musing!"

And so the book was published. There appeared a great number of books, similar to each other. All of them were spread around the world. You got one. A Mom and her Kid are reading the other one. You will learn what they are musing over. And you yourself can think together with them, and with your relatives. With anyone you want or like.

A story about bricks

In a box on a shelf there lived some toy bricks. And they wanted desperately to become a tower.

— Well, tomorrow morning we'll already be a tower, — thought the bricks every single evening. But tomorrow, and the day after tomorrow and day after every day the bricks still stayed at the same place — in the box on the shelf.

One day a woman who lived in that house was dusting the shelves and happened to drop the box, and the bricks fell down.

— Oh! Now we're going to make a tower!

But it was not to be. The bricks plonked onto the floor far from each other. And they did not happen to make a tower.

But then in came a Builder. He was already four years old. He was also Connector and Creator. He thought for a moment and then he put the bricks like this:

The tower was built.

And now...

A-musing!

(If something is inventive, there must be an inventor.)

— But what can I muse over? And what is so interesting about this story: a boy has made a tower of bricks — that's all!

— Right! How many times do you have to drop the box of bricks from the shelf to make them become a tower?

— They are not likely to become a tower on the first try. Maybe you'll have to drop them about fifteen times, maybe more, and maybe they will never become a tower at all...

— Why do you think so?

— Well, 'cos bricks are not actually alive, they can't agree with each other how they should stand.

— Obviously not. So there must be someone who would imagine the whole tower, and then would carefully put the bricks on their places. You know it yourself — you play with bricks quite often. Well, I came to your room recently and there was a castle that you'd built. It was so inventive.

— You mean it was invented by me?

— This is almost the same.

I was standing there looking at your palace: where you'd put the columns, where you'd constructed an arch, where you'd made windows. I imagined how you had been inventing and building all that. As if I was partly with you when you were building the palace.

— Wow! That's amazing! I was not there, but you seemed to be with me. How did you do that?

— The thing is that when I'm thinking of something complicated and beautiful, I'm also thinking about the person who has created it.

One day I went to an exhibition of lace. What weaved figures, flowers and butterflies were there! To weave them you had to make thousands of eyelets, thousands of beads, and all of them in their own places, you had to imagine at the beginning how it would look in the end. I was admiring those patterns and it felt as if I was looking at the delicate fingers of the lace-maker, following her imagination, watching her creating the beauty. I had never met that woman, but when I was looking at the lace, my soul met her soul.

— Mom, but it's such a joy — to feel someone you don't see like this. And what story will the a-musing book tell next?

— The next story is about an apple seed.

— And what can be told about it, I wonder?

A story about an apple seed

Once upon a time there lived an apple seed — a brown and smooth one.

And one day, there came noise: «chomp-chomp»

— Someone's eating my apple, my little home! — the seed realized in horror.

And the next moment it found itself on a child's palm. One little movement — and the seed fell onto the soft ground in the garden.

Many days passed. And suddenly, the seed felt something moving inside itself, some strange urge.

A gentle sprout moved the earth and looked at the sunlight.

Here they are: the air, the sun, the world!

Everything around it was full of desire to live and to grow.

Time passed. First the sprout turned into a supple twig. And the plant then turned into... Do you know what the plant turned into?

A-musing!

(There is a creator of the world.)

— Well, I know it. The apple seed will grow into an apple tree. But how can such a small seed keep a whole tree inside?

— You mean, where does the material for the tree come from?

— Well, yeah.

— At first the seed took all the elements necessary for the sprout from itself. And afterwards, when there appeared little roots, it became possible to borrow all the elements from the earth. In the roots elements transformed into the others. It happened because the particles of the substances were rearranged to make new substances. And so the apple tree was constructed.

— It' just like bricks, isn't it?

— Right. But there are more particles then bricks in any box. There are millions of millions of them.

— How hard it must *be* to arrange them! Surely, the particles can't get together themselves. Someone who has gathered them must *be* very smart and very strong! Do you remember telling me that when we are watching the things, we are getting closer to the people who have made them? But there is no such person who has made the seed, but I feel I've got closer to Someone great, alive and very, very light. It's God, isn't it, Mom?

— Yes, it is God, everyone who feels Him is very happy.

— And when did you feel him?

— Do you remember our canoe trip? You used to wonder then why I was silent. And I was looking at the river, at the flecks of light on the golden sand. I saw the weed crawling, the silver fish passing by. You know, even if a scientist was given all the bones, scales and finlets, and was provided all the necessary equipment, they wouldn't *be* able to make such living fish. And they would also have to create those substances, which the fish's organs are made of.

— So, why were you silent then?

— Because I didn't want to lose closeness to the One Who has created the fish, the weed and the sand, the willows, their leaves, the earth, the green carpet of grass, the flowers, the bumble-bees, the birds and the grasshoppers. I felt the same Light, the same Mind that has created them all, united them and existed in them. That's how you can feel God by looking at everything that exists is in the forest, in the field, and in the sea. In everything that exists on our planet. You can feel God in the movement of stars and planets, in the whole endless space.

A story about a magnet

In a drawer of father's desk there lived a magnet. Months have passed since he was last taken out, so he was bored. Because most of all he loved to draw all kinds of metal things, so that they jumped and stuck to him.

At last there came a squeak, the drawer was pulled out of the desk, and the magnet found himself in the little, strong and scratched hands of a boy. The magnet felt at once that these were the hands of a real Discoverer and Explorer, the one who is already four years old.

Those hands put the magnet onto the table. Now he was happy. The little Explorer played all sorts of games with the magnet, he had tried to draw all kinds of things with it.

— And what if the magnet pulled a needle, and a thread didn't let it go? — suddenly wondered the Explorer. He grabbed a needle, tied it by the thread to the back of a chair, and slowly moved the magnet close to it. And that's where the most interesting thing happened.

A-musing!

(There are invisible things)

— What happened next?

— Well, why should we talk about it, we'd rather make the same experiment ourselves...

Hop! — the needle jumped to the magnet, but couldn't reach it and froze, hanging in the air. The thread didn't swag as if it was not a thread but another thin steel needle.

— That's how a magnet can hold a needle.

— Is it holding it? Here, look at me, I put my finger there and I can't feel anything.

— Of course you can't. For it's a magnetic force, and you can't touch it.

— What is this magnetic force? Not only can't I feel anything there, I can't see anything either!

— And you won't see it. For it's invisible.

— Well, it's kind of... there's nothing there and still there is something. It's sort of really weird. And is there anything invisible apart from magnetic force?

— Sure, there are lots of things. And there are even invisible things that are living.

— And what are they?

— Well that's easy. Our thoughts, our love, kindness, joy, excitement. Has anyone held them in their hands, touched or see them? Are they made of some kind of material? No. But we can feel them quite distinctly. And if you X-ray a person you will see lungs and heart. But you won't see joy. And a surgeon, making a surgery, never sees neither love nor hatred in a man, neither bravery nor cowardice, neither generosity nor greed. But they all exist. 'Cos these words were not made in vain. All those things are invisible and immaterial.

— Mom, and is it true then that brain and thoughts are not the same?

— It is definitely true. As a radio is not the same as radio waves.

— Mom, I think, I'm going to understand something really important right now. We can't see God either, but we feel Him... Maybe it's because He is not like a man with head and body. He must be like invisible Love or invisible Joy, and He has neither size nor substance, neither shape nor figure...

A story about a dress

Once upon a time there lived a dress. How happy the girl was, when she was given that dress as a birthday present. You bet, she was! How lovely, how delicately was it made, how beautifully decorated! The girl put it on at once and began to receive guests. And the guests congratulated the girl, told her a lot of nice things and gave her presents. Only the dress didn't notice the girl. And how could it? It was the girl who was wearing the dress, and the dress was on her body. So the dress thought that all those nice and warm words were said to it, that it was the dress, who got all those presents. The dress felt that it was a very important person.

— To be a person means to have nice little pockets with sparkling buttons, pleats on the skirt and coloured ribbons...

A-musing!

(A person is not just a body but also a soul)

— Anyone can understand that... A person is not buttons and pleats. A girl is a person.

— And where is the girl's personality? Is it her head? Her arms? Or her legs?

— No, of course not her arms and legs...

— Do you remember us talking about the invisible things in the world? Well there are such things inside us too.

— Oh, I see! It's a soul!

— Yes, it is. When a man dies, the soul leaves the body and looks at it from the outside, as if it were clothes that had been taken off. The man no longer has a body, but he still exists.

— And I think I've just realized something about God. He doesn't have a body, He doesn't have arms or legs like we do. But He loves us, He holds the world. He is a Spirit, but still He is like a person not like air or magnetic force. And it's our soul that resembles God, not our body. But in a human soul there is good and evil. And there is nothing evil about God — just good.

A story about matryoshka dolls

One day a matryoshka doll was brought to a toy store. She was taken out of the box and put into a show-case among the other toys.

— Well, here I am! Let's be friends, — matryoshka smiled to a stacking toy, a wound-up lorry and a white furry rabbit.

— Pleased to have you in our company, — nodded the stacking toy greeting her. —You've got such a gorgeous blue varnished kerchief.

— What are you talking about? I'm wearing a red kerchief. Look, this is me! — the toys heard a voice talking. This voice was smaller, it came from the inside of the matryoshka with a blue kerchief.

Suddenly, the matryoshka with a *blue* kerchief opened. And a matryoshka in a red kerchief appeared in front of the toys. And she cried immediately:

— This is me!

The toys were very surprised:

— And we thought that the matryoshka with the *blue* kerchief should say «me» about herself, and it turns out that the inner matryoshka has right to say «me».

But then out of the red matryoshka came another one, with a green kerchief and certainly she also exclaimed «This is me!»

— So this is she, this is our real guest, this is the third matryoshka, and the first and the second ones are nothing but her clothes. It's right that she calls herself «me».

Then the fourth matryoshka appeared. Her kerchief was bright yellow. The toys were really confused now. All three matryoshkas had turned out to be clothes. And the real person, calling herself «me» was this one, the fourth matryoshka. But this time the toys didn't rush to say hello.

They doubtfully looked at the matryoshka with a yellow kerchief. Won't there be another one? Another «me»? And there she came, of course: an absolutely tiny one with an orange kerchief.

— Open up quickly, you also can't call yourself «me», — hurried up the stacking toy.

— I can't, I'm made of one solid piece of wood, I won't open. I do not consist of parts, I mean, I'm really simple. That's who I am.

— She is the real matryoshka's self, she can say «me» about her herself, — admitted all the toys.

A-musing!

(What is "me"?)

— It resembles the story about a dress a little bit. There was also a dress that thought it was a person, but the dress was taken off and it was the girl who turned out to be a person. And here there were lots of things that had to be taken off.

— Well, yes, of course they are alike. Both stories — the story about a dress and the story about matryoshkas — are the stories about people.

— I got it, I got it! In the clothes there is a man, and in the man's body there is a soul. Like in one matryoshka there is another one, and in that one — there is one more. So, is our soul — that very last matryoshka and there is nothing that lies deeper than she does?

— No, deeper than soul lies spirit. Soul and spirit are not the same things.

— And how do they differ?

— Well, let's look at ourselves: who are we talking about when we say "me"?.. I'm saying: "This is me". I'm looking at myself: I'm wearing a dark skirt, a lacy blouse, and I understand that clothes is just an outer envelope, my self is observing this envelope from the inside. But I can also say: "This is a scar from the cut on my finger, but it's already healing. My throat hurts a bit (we've eaten too much ice-cream)". So my body also seems to be an envelope which my inner self can look at from the inside. And I also can say: "I'm happy" or "I'm scared" or "I'm angry" or "I love". So there turns out to be someone deep inside us who is also watching what's happening in our souls.

— So, does that mean that the soul is an outer envelope too?

— Yes, it looks like thoughts and feelings are also some sort of clothes for the one who is speaking about them from the inside, from the ultimate depth. A man has got thoughts and feeling but they are not the same as his self.

We're doing quite an interesting thing now: as if we were stripping the cabbage leaf by leaf. The cabbage has got many layers, many envelopes. And in a man's soul you can find different layers, different levels. And many people feel that there is a real inner self, which is the main thing in a person. But no one really understands what this self is like.

— But why?

— Because there is no one deeper who could name this self.

— And the same is with God, remember: we also can't tell who God is. So does that mean that God and our deepest depth are alike?

— Yes, they are. And not only can we look for God around us, but also inside ourselves.

— And I was told, that it's bad to be selfish. There's no "i" in "team".

— That's absolutely different. You were told about the passion of vanity, it's a very bad feeling. And now we are taking about a true real human self. It looks at all our feelings, but it is not equal to any of them. It chooses among the feelings, it lies at the very center of the soul.

— How can we call the one who is in the centre, the one who chooses?

— The one who is in the centre has many names: the Image of God, God's voice in a man, consciousness, true self (it has nothing to do with being selfish or boastful). Besides, there is a difference in the Bible between man's soul and spirit. Thoughts and feelings belong to soul. And spirit is the centre. But there is no word to describe the whole essence of the one who lies in the centre.

— But why?

— Because the centre is not a thought or a feeling. And you'll understand it better when you read the other stories.

A note for parents. About the difference between man's soul and spirit.

"...it is sown a natural body, it is raised a spiritual body. If there is a natural body, there is also a spiritual body. So it is written: "The first man Adam became a living being" ; the last Adam, a life-giving spirit. The spiritual did not come first, but the natural, and after that the spiritual. The first man was of the dust of the earth; the second man is of heaven". (Cor 15:44-47 Holman Christian Standard Bible (HCSB))

"Then the Lord God formed a man from the dust of the ground and breathed into his nostrils the breath of life, and the man became a living being". (Ge 2:7 New International Version)

A story about dew

One day dew fell on the meadow — lots and lots of tiny dewdrops. It happened in the evening when the sun had already set, so the dewdrops had never seen the sun yet. Night fell. Stars appeared in the dark sky.

— The stars are sparkling in the sky so beautifully! Like fireflies in the grass near us, — the old moon heard a loud whisper. She was already two days old.

— Hey, who's talking the stars up here? — the moon grumbled.

— We are, — the frightened dewdrops answered.

— So, I guess you're too young yet and you haven't seen the real beauty. Wait till the sun rises and you'll know what the real blaze and glory are.

— And what is the sun? — curious dewdrops wondered.

— How can I explain it? When it appears you'll understand yourself what's what.

Time passed and the dewdrops were still waiting for the sun. Then the night passed, the sky turned rosy, and at last sparkling and gleaming the sun rose. As soon as the world was filled with sunlight the dewdrops felt that something good was happening to everything around them.

— Look! It's the sun! — a puddle exclaimed. But the dewdrops couldn't get where to look. They were confused, for there was one huge sun shining in the sky, but there were also thousands of little suns sparkling in the dewdrops on the meadow.

— Each one of you is a little mirror for the Sun. Lots of tiny sparks are reflections of the big Sun in you. The Sun is shining in all of you, because it exists beyond you, — explained the puddle.

A-musing!

(there is an image of God in a man)

— I feel so good that I don't even want to think, I want to feel the same as the dewdrops did.

— And you are really just like them.

— I am like a dewdrop? Am I sort of little, round and liquid?

— Oh, no, definitely not. That's not what I mean.

— And what do you mean? Why are we alike?

— Our souls are also mirrors for God, like the dewdrops are the mirrors for the Sun.

There are many people in the world and in each soul there is a mysterious "self". This "self" is like a spark in a dewdrop. This "self" is also like the smallest matryoshka having no other matryoshkas inside. Many-many "selves" of all people are the reflections of the one and the same Higher "Self".

— And who is this Higher Self?

— Of course, it's God!

— It's just so unusual, that you've called God "the Higher Self". I've never heard it before. What did you mean?

— That God is the nameless personal Beginning of everything.

— Wow! What clever words! And what does that mean?

— That means that God is a personality, He is alive, He is conscious of Himself, He can say "Me" about Himself.

— Why is the Beginning nameless?

— Because before God there had been no one, no one could have given Him a name. It was God who called everything in the world to life by giving names to all things.

— I got it! I got it! That's why the very centre of my soul can't be named either — because it's a reflection of God who has no name.

A note for the grown-ups. It would be good if a grown-up who is talking to a child also told them about how often the image of the God is mistaken for similar appearance, and how people sometimes think that God looks like a human being, which is wrong. You should remind them, that a body is actually a characteristic of a man. Remind them, that God is a disembodied spirit.

Sometimes we also hear the ideas that God lives only in a human being and nowhere else. These are the ideas of man being a god and they leave humans in hopeless isolation in the empty Universe. And it's very important to tell in more details that God is able to shine in a man, like the sun shines in the dew-drops, because He exists outside people, in all times and dimensions.

The words about God being a nameless Beginning is also a topic for an inspiring and uplifting talk. There is an interesting and helpful mathematical example: a zero standing in the centre of coordinates system. Two coordinates are reckoned from zero and a point is put down on a plane. We may say that by naming the coordinates, by using the words the zero creates the point. All the endless plane is made of numerous points, created by the zero, created by zero naming them, defining them by coordinates. Zero is not an empty space, it's not nothing. It contains everything in it, all infinite aggregate of points that make a plane. Zero itself is a starting point, it can't be reckoned from any other point.

The fact that by naming other points the zero creates them, makes it present on every eternal plane. It is everywhere in this eternity and it holds it in itself.

A story about a hare

Once upon a time there lived a little hare. To tell the truth he hadn't yet lived long — he was just beginning to live. He had just been born and was looking around in amazement trying to understand what it was all around him and what was it called. The little hare looked up.

— It's the sky, — said his mother-hare.

And unfortunately at that very moment an ugly black cloud covered the sky.

— Oh, how scary this sky is, — squeaked the hare.

— No, the sky is not scary. It's the cloud that is, — tried to explain mother-hare.

But the little hare couldn't understand it for all he saw was the cloud, and he couldn't imagine the sky without it. He understood everything only when the wind drove the cloud away and the sky beamed at the little hare. Since then every time when the clouds covered the sky, the hare bravely shouted at them:

— I'm not afraid of you, I know that you are in the sky, but you are not the sky. You'll go away, and the sky itself is kind, clear and nice.

A-musing!

(The difference between spirit, passions and good feelings in a man's soul)

— Clouds are like bad feelings in our soul, like passions as they are also called. Like a cloud that sometimes can cover the whole sky, a passion can fill the soul. And so the man would feel as if that passion and he himself were the same. Clouds-passions hide in our soul. They have names: Arrogance, Vanity, Greed, Laziness, Sloth. When a man himself chooses some of them he becomes like them. There are also beautiful colorful clouds — good feelings. Their names are: Joy, Love, Kindness, Bravery, Generosity. Every now and then one of them spreads all over the soul.

— And who makes the choice?

— Man's real self. Not something that resembles ugly or beautiful clouds — but something that resembles the sky.

— We've already talked a lot about the real «self» of a man. We called it the image of God, compared it to sunshine in a dewdrop, to the smallest matryoshka. And now you've found a good comparison to the sky. A cloud might not see or know the sky, it knows only itself, but the sky knows the cloud and knows that it can get free of the cloud.

The same is with a man. For example he may be taken by a passion of anger. If he remembers that he is not the anger himself and tells in his soul: "I am in great anger", by naming it he would free himself from this bad feeling. Because as he can name it, this means he is not the feeling himself. Like the sky is not the same as the cloud. That's how you can turn from feeling a passion to sensing the image of God. It's the beginning of repentance, the beginning of victory over passion and sin. It's a shame when people think that their greed, anger and vanity are their selves, when they keep and defend passions. That is selfishness — the sin of self-loving.

When one loves the true base of themselves, clear sky, and wants the clouds not to spoil it — it's the real high love of yourself, of the image of God. I think that is the love Christ was talking about: "love thy neighbor as thyself" (Matthew 19:19 King James Bible).

A story about a washing machine

A new washing machine was brought into a flat. She hadn't yet have time to meet all her new neighbors — the ones living in the bathroom: taps and a bath, a sink and a mirror — and she was already filled with clothes and wash powder and turned on. The washing machine grumbled and crackled.

— What are you doing? Why are you making that noise? — the mirror asked her. He was very curious and reflected everything in himself.

— Can't you *see*, I'm washing the clothes?

— What do you mean you are washing the clothes? It's people's job — to wash the clothes. How many times have I watched the mistress rubbing it in the bath with her soft hands, and you — you even don't have hands! Just something *bubbling* and turning inside you. No, you can't *be* washing without a human.

— No matter, what you think. I am automatic! And I am perfectly fine with doing everything on my own. So it's me who is washing, and humans have nothing to do with it.

The mirror went silent in astonishment. He carefully watched the clothes being taken out of the machine, and looked at what was inside her.

He spoke again only when people left.

— And could you please tell me, — he asked the machine. — What do you need all those wires, pipes, wheels and buttons for?

— Ha-ha-ha, — laughed the machine with contempt. — What a *stupid* glass! How can you make out my mechanism. You haven't got one yourself, and my buttons, wires and wheels are connected with each other in a way that makes them move, and this is how the washing is done.

— Well, I see, — the mirror continued thoughtfully. — So, the man who constructed you made your mechanism so that moving it would do the washing. So, making you, that man already foresaw all your washing and somehow did it with you. You are only an instrument. And though it *seems* as if you were washing yourself, the fact is that a man is washing with you.

A-musing!

(the things that God is doing with nature)

— Mom, you know, I wanted to show Igor, how I can *see* things differently now.

— What do you mean?

— Well, I mean, to look at a tree and not only *see* it but also feel that it was created by God.

— So, what about Igor?

— You know what, it was such a shame: he didn't feel or understand anything. He said: "Why do you keep making these God things up! It's a *seed*, the tree has grown from. And it's nothing to do with God!"

— Ah, I *see*... Like many grown up people, Igor thinks that everything that appears in nature is made by nature itself, without any participation of God. So many people choose who has created everything: God or nature. But why should we choose? We don't have to choose if the clothes is washed by the automatic washing machine or by a man, do we?

— I got it, I got it! God creates things by nature just like a man washes by a washing machine.

— Of course He does! The powers of nature, the laws of nature are invented by God. And then they make a great lot of things. Nature is an instrument for God. Machines work without man's help, but still a man acts through them. When something is born in nature by the force of nature is happens by the will of God, so the God acts although we do not see Him.

A story about river sand

On the bank of the river there lived clean yellow sand. Around him the sparrows were twittering something to one another, the grass was whispering quietly, but the sand himself could not speak.

One day the sand was taken to a yard and put into a sand-pit.

The sand was happy: he hoped that at last he wouldn't be so lonely.

And he was right: a boy came up to the sand-pit. He put his little hands into the sand, and under his touch the sand began to turn into galleries, walls and underground tunnels.

— What a great castle it is! — the sand thought happily. — And I know everything about this fortress; I know what it was like in the boy's imagination. I know every single little detail of it, for he has created this fantasy with the help of my flesh. I've become the body for his thoughts. He is speaking through me. And this language has the easiest words to understand.

A-musing!

(Triune God)

— Why is it said here that a sand fortress is a word? You know, the words we speak — they are made of sounds. And if we write them, they are made of letters. Well, everyone knows that, we studied it at school.

— But still there are not only the words we pronounce.

— And what else?

— Music is a word, a painting is a word, a house is a word. Every thing made by a man is his word.

— How can that be?

— Well, let's think... A word is what people use to name something, to express something. They look at the scarlet sky and say: it is sunset. But sometimes a man can feel that one word is not enough to name something — that it can't express all the beauty of what they see.

Then the man takes photos of the sunset or paints a picture or composes music. These are words too. All those invisible and beautiful things that the man wanted to say about the sunset are expressed on the canvass or in the tune.

A word is a material form of sense. A form can be made of sounds when we pronounce words or of paints when we draw, or of shape when we make sculptures or construct buildings.

— It seems that there is nothing in the world but words. Do you mean that the world itself is a word too?

— Yes, it is. The whole world is the Word of God. That's clear. If a human self, that is the image of God, like sparks of sun in dewdrops, can bring meaning into life using words, then God must be the first one to do it.

— And do you remember reading to me the Gospel which said: "in the beginning was the Word" (John 1:1 (American Standart))?

— That means that God has created the world with His Word.

God wanted something to exist — and so it appeared. It appeared because He brought it to life, drew it out of Himself, like a word. When something appears in the world that means that He has spoken His word. God wanted the world to be what it is, and embodying His conception, matter appeared, atoms connected to each other, planets were born and stars began to shine, rivers ran across the surface of the Earth, plants and animals inhabited it. Imagine a happy poet, who is full of new ideas, he expresses what is straining at the leash, and it's not his voice sounding, these are not verses lying down on the paper — these are real things, actions, events appearing in the world. All of this is a material word...

God who is over all, He, whom we can't name, but who can say "Me" about Himself — He is God the Father.

His external aspect is God the Son. He is a Word born from the Father, from the Thought.

Everything created by God is alive and continues to live in posterity. The miraculous power of life in every creature is the Holy Spirit. He constantly revives and moves everything in the world.

I've just told you about the Holy Trinity: the Father, the Son and the Holy Spirit.

— I've seen such icon: there were three angels sitting at the table. And I thought there is only one God.

— But there is One, right you are. And you yourself are also the one and only, though we can find three yous: there is inner intention, a vague thought, a word that embodies that thought, and you yourself, living and containing life inside you. So, there are three, but you are only one human being.

It's wrong to think about Trinity as a family if three. There are three angels on the icon because it's impossible to paint the "Self", the Original Being, the Word and Life.

Note for the grown-ups: St. Gregory The Theologian says: "A thought was a deed that was performed by Word and fulfilled by Spirit." (The statement of St. Gregory is not a sacred script, since it is a philosopher of later times.)

A story about a lathe

On a factory in a workshop there lived some lathes. Every morning workers came and stood at their lathes. Every worker worked only at his own lathe, knew everything about it and managed to operate it.

At night when the lathes were turned off they were sleeping and dreaming. And one night one of the lathes dreamt that the workers gathered in the morning but didn't want to work. Only Vasily Afanasievich tried to persuade everyone to stay and work.

"If you want to work then stay here alone and look after the lathes", — decided the other workers.

So Vasily Afanasievich was left alone. The lathes were making noise, rattling and clattering all around.

Suddenly one of the lathes broke, Vasily Afanasievich ran up to it. He barely started to fix it when there came some alarm signals from two more lathes. And poor Vasily Afanasievich couldn't figure out where to run first. So he slammed the door and went out. And afterwards he explained everything to other workers like this: "Well, I can't be in all places at a time, can I? I can't see and hear everything and keep everything in order on my own!"

A-musing!

(The God is everywhere and He holds everything)

— And how can God do it? For He has to sustain life, connections and movement in all the worlds, in all big and little things that inhabit those worlds.

— So how does He manage to do that? I've no idea.

— I'll tell you... He has time to do everything not because He flies so quickly from one place to another, but because He is everywhere at the same time. There isn't a place without Him.

— How can that be, Mom? I can't be walking in the street and studying at school at the same time, can I?

— Of course, you can't, because your body can be only in one place at a time. But God doesn't have a body that people have...

— Then maybe He is so big, that He spreads around like heat of a radiator or light of a lamp?

— No, He doesn't. Heat and electricity are both only creations of God, His deeds, and it's not right to compare them to the Living God the Creator. God is Life itself.

He thinks, he feels happiness, love and care. And one more thing: light and heat spread their particles over the world. And God is whole in everything — big or little — in every place of the universe at the same time.

— Well, mom, that is totally baffling, there's no way for me to understand it.

— Looks like we'll need another example to help you understand. Imagine a teacher: she is standing at her desk (in one place), but her "Self" is connected to all children in the classroom. And at the same time it is connected to her own children — they are little and they are waiting for her at home. And her "self" is also connected to her friends and relatives. Her "self" does not divide into parts, does not fly from one person to another. It stays whole with everyone she loves. Remember us talking about God being the Higher "Self"? So no wonder that He can be everywhere. And we can say about Him: God the Spirit is Omnipresent.

A story. In turn or all together

One day, the Explorer — the one who is already four years old — had to make quite a hard choice. He had just had breakfast and was thinking what toy he would play with. On the table in front of him there stood a wound-up train, a soldier and a little fluffy dog.

The kid made a reach for one of the toys but suddenly he felt that each of them wanted to be with him. He couldn't dare take one of them for that would have hurt the other two. The train was at his left, and the kid put his palms on both sides of it. He watched the train standing between his palms.

— So, now the train is in front of me, now we are together, the two of us, — thought the kid. — And I shall look at the soldier and the dog later, that will only happen in the future.

The kid put his palms on both sides of the soldier, and now the soldier was in the "present". The train stayed in the past and the dog was waiting for him in the future.

Then the kid watched the dog standing between his palms, and it was in the present. The train and the soldier stayed in the past.

Suddenly, the kid took his hands off the table and all three toys were in front of his eyes; the past and the future united in the present. All three toys stayed with the boy: he united them all with his attention.

A-musing

(God is eternal)

— I know you've told me this story for a reason. You are going to tell me something clever about God, aren't you?

— Right you are. My story is not about the boy being able to see several toys at a time. It's about the ability of God to embrace all the time: the past, the present and the future. There are no past or future for Him. There is only present.

— I can't get it. Well, two years ago I got a teddy-bear as a present from you and Dad. How happy was I then! But I can't go back to that moment now, it's passed and it's gone.

— It is for you, yes. But for God everything exists right now: this conversation we are having with you, the presenting of that bear, and that time, when you were born, and when we, your parents were little, and when your grannies and grandpas were born, and when our planet appeared and when our Universe was created.

— Do you mean that God has got a Time machine and can travel to the past and to the future?

— No, God does not travel. He is in all times and places simultaneously. Same as the boy's attention stayed with the train, the soldier and the dog and embraced them not one by one, but all together.

— I think I understand. We live our days one by one, and God takes them all together. That must *be* because we are small and He is endlessly great. And all that has already happened and is yet to come lies in front of Him. I wonder if God knows what I will do when I grow up.

— Not only does He know, but He already exists in the things that only lie ahead of us. All your life and the life of your children and grandchildren are now in front of Him. He is with them, and what for us is future for Him is present. All those moments that go far back into the past and far away into the future are present for Him. That's what eternity is. There is only present in eternity.

God is eternal.

— So, Mom, you say that God was before all and created everything. And who had been before God and had created Him?

— If there had been anyone before God it's he, whom we should have called "god". And then you would ask who had created him and called the next one "god", and asked who had created him, and so on. This line with no beginning would go on and on back into the past. And you want to feel the One who has always existed in this distance with neither beginning nor end.

But this *is* God Himself, God the Creator, God the Pantocrator. He has no beginning, which means he is eternal. He has always been and he will always be, however many millions of years pass. And you have no need to think of the other one, two or three persons who had been before Him. And there's no point in asking when God appeared, in trying to place His beginning in some moment of time. For He didn't appear in some moment of time, but He himself created the time like He created space.

A story about caterpillars

One day two caterpillars crawled into a greenhouse.

— Look, there's a gardener, — one of them whispered to the other.

— Aye, well... Those gardeners are all like this: just waiting to poison you or make some other hideous thing up...

— How can a gardener know that we are not just eating the fruits. We are going to chew them for an important scientific purpose.

— Yeah, we'll try all fruits and learn which one is the best, the tastiest and the finest.

And then for quite a long time whispering and champing could be heard from under the leaves.

— Here, I think I've found it. This pear is the sweetest and the most delicious one.

— No. That apple should be sweeter and tastier.

— Look, we haven't tried that peach yet.

A-musing!

(Forbidden fruit is sweet)

— Oh, Mom, they are going to gnaw the greenhouse all over. And they still won't find that fruit, because the most delicious fruit was in the Garden of Eden, in paradise. But I don't know, what kind of fruit was that.

— It must have been neither an apple nor a pear. Most likely the so called forbidden fruit was a bad action, a sin forbidden by God.

— What do you mean?

— I'll tell you... Imagine you've heard Misha stuttering and wanted to mock him... And then there is that moment when you choose either to say something mocking or to stay silent. If you mock him, you would do something that God has forbidden. And so you'd pick up a forbidden fruit. And if you say nothing the forbidden fruit would stay untouched. Or for no good reason you may want to throw a stone at a cat. And again you have this moment of making a choice: to give in to temptation and throw a stone, or to resist the temptation and walk away. This how the forbidden fruit can be a bad action and not a fruit.

— So, if a time machine took us back into a moment, when the first people made the first sin we would see a completely different thing from what they draw on the pictures, where Eve hands an apple to Adam?

— It might be so...

— How could that be?! For Granny told me that the first people had become bad because they had eaten the forbidden fruit; that means that the fruit had brought evil into their hearts.

— Well, imagine a similar situation. A mother told to her son: "Here, I've bought a cake, soon the guests will come and we'll eat it together". A boy was strolling around the table, looking at the cake, and then couldn't resist and bit a piece. And so he is looking at that bitten cake and thinking: what mom would say? And he's feeling himself so unpleasant, uncomfortable and somewhat miserable. So how can that come: the cake is good and nice but something disgusting has penetrated into the soul.

— Clearly, the evil didn't get into the soul from the cake. The boy feels bad because he has done what his mother had forbidden, he's let her down, and she can be mad with him.

— Now that means that evil gets into the soul with bad actions, with sins. And there are many such bad actions which do not involve eating anything, but the soul is still aching and getting dark. This happens when a man lies, boasts, swears, betrays someone, when he is greedy or behaves like a coward. There are so many such things... All of them are forbidden by God, and all of them are forbidden fruits.

A story about a robot

There was a robot in the toy store. He was constructed to resemble a human in every way. You could program him as you wanted.

— I am a good and exciting toy, — thought the robot. — I wish I was given to a boy, who wouldn't get bored with me, who wouldn't break me or throw me away.

Then a day came when robot heard a shop-assistant talking about him to two people: a boy and his Dad.

The shop-assistant was recommending the robot, and the boy told to his dad:

— That's exactly what I need; he is totally like a man, and he's going to be my friend. So I can do without Valerka. For, you know: I call him to go for a walk with me — and he doesn't want to. I ask him to let me play with his ball — and he never lets me. I don't want a friend like this! I can live without him. The robot is much better.

Do you think the robot was happy to hear that? Nothing of the kind, he was frightened: "That's it. I'm done for. I can only be a toy — and not a friend. Very soon the boy will realize it, and he'll break and throw me away though it is none of my fault."

But who cares what robots may think. The father went to pay, and the shop-assistant packed the robot in a nice box...

Back at home the boy's parents helped him to program the robot; so that he knew what to say, what to do, what games to play. Every morning as soon as the boy woke up, he ran fast to his new toy. But already a few days later his parents noticed that the boy was spending less and less time with his robot.

— Now, are you already bored with the friend we've bought you? — his Dad asked.

— He is not a friend at all, is he? I always know in advance, what he's going to answer or to do, for it was I who programmed him. To play with him is the same as to play alone, be on my own. I wish I could make peace with Valerka!

— But Valerka doesn't always agree with you, sometimes he is greedy, he often argues and even fights with you.

— I don't care. But then, when he's nice to me — it is real, and I actually have a friend.

So was the robot eventually thrown away? Of course, not. When the boy made peace with his friend the robot became very useful!

A-musing!

(God never forced man to be good, He gave him a choice)

— Some people wonder, why God had to plant such a dangerous tree in His garden? For if He is in the future as well as in the present, He knew in advance that people won't be able to resist the temptation.

— Mom, but you've told me yourself that there might not have been such tree, and the forbidden fruit was just a man's choice — to listen to the God's will or to act differently.

— Aye, a man is not like a robot with one single program, he is like a Knight with the parting of the ways ahead of him. But there is still a question. Instead of "Why did God plant that tree" we can ask: "Why did God let man make his own choice between good and evil?"

— Hold on, but how could it not be like that? Well, you know, if we didn't makes choices I can't even imagine what people would be like.

— That's it, if God had programmed people to be kind, they wouldn't have been people, they would have been robots. And they wouldn't be able to become God's friends when they enter the eternal life in Heaven.

A story about a beautiful park

One small nice and tidy park loved his frequent visitor very much. That was an elder thoughtful man.

— I can feel his life and he can feel mine, — thought the park joyfully. — I know, that when he leaves he takes home with him the sun twinkles of my leaves, the smell of my flowerbeds, the shade of my alleys.

— It's nice here, — said the man. — It's a corner of paradise.

But one day the man came to the park in bad mood: he was frowning, his eyes were full of tears, and his lips — pressed into a thin line.

Slumping, he sat in his usual place close to a calm pond.

— Today is one of the most beautiful days of the summer, and I can't give this beauty to my friend, — thought the park desperately. — My sunlight, my bright colours can't reach his soul, that is full of pain.

— The park doesn't make me feel happy today, — said the man when he was leaving. Today it's not as nice as always. And it surely is far from paradise.

A-musing!

(What does the banishment from Heaven mean)

— Mom, look at this picture in the children's Bible: sad Adam and Eve are wandering through a dark forest. That must be after God has banished them from paradise, right? And where are they going from, and where to? Where was the paradise situated, and where did they move to? From Heaven to Earth? Or from a nice place on the Earth to a worse one?

— The Bible says that the paradise was situated between the rivers Tigris and Euphrates. These two rivers still exist. Although I think that the banishment from paradise did not necessarily mean going by foot from one place to another. It might just as well be like staying in one's favourite park but being incapable to embrace its beauty because the soul is full of pain.

The souls of those first people had turned dark because they were ashamed for their sin. The paradise didn't reflect in them anymore. So they could see the paradise from the outside because they didn't have it inside them.

— It looks like they'd banished themselves from heaven?

— Looks like it.

— Then, I'd drew the banishment from paradise like this: Fist I'd show a garden reflected in a clear soul, and then — in a dark one.

A story about a teapot

A little teapot had a bright pattern on his white sides. And he was cheerful and friendly. He loved standing on the table and having tea with people. He always *bubbled delightfully*, when hot and nosey tea poured through his spout into people's cups.

But one day the teapot got scared.

He saw a new person at the table. It was a child, who was yet less than a year old. He was sitting on his mother's lap, waving his hands chaotically, grabbing and moving different objects.

— Oh, he's going to grab me, the boiling water will pour out and he'll burn himself! — gasped the teapot in silent horror. He wished so much he could move away and escape the baby hands.

But the mother moved the teapot away herself and said a couple of time:

— It's hot. You can't touch it. It's hot.

So it happened again and again. Every time the child was at the table, he tried to touch the hot teapot. And his Mom kept saying: "It's hot!"

— Why doesn't he get such a simple word — "hot", — thought the teapot sadly. He tried to be more careful, but still one little hot drop fell on to the child's hand. The boy burst out crying and his mother quickly poured cold water on the red spot and went on saying: "Oi, oi, It hurts! It's hot!"

The next time as soon as mother said: "Don't touch it, it's hot!" — the kid jerked back his hand at once and even moved away from the teapot.

A-musing!

(Why the tree in paradise was called the tree of knowledge of good and evil)

— I've understood everything in this story. Before the child felt heat he hadn't understood the word "hot", it was hollow for him. These were just some meaningless sounds. And when he actually burnt himself he did realize what feeling is meant by the word "hot".

— And how do you think, which words were meaningless for Adam and Eve?

— Oh, I see! Like that kid, who'd never burnt himself, the first people had never been hurt, insulted, beaten or deceived. And they'd never done such things to anyone.

— Exactly! So, for them the words "bad", "lie", "pain", "offense", "deceit", "grief", "greed", "shame" were hollow and lacking any kind of actual feeling. Put simply, they didn't know evil. And after their bad deed, they felt the taste of it. They learnt what evil meant. That's why the tree is called "The tree of knowledge of good and evil".

— But before people there had been animals that had killed and eaten each other.

— Yes, there were. But only people have the mysterious "Self" in them, the image of God, that deep inside can feel and judge what is evil. So there appeared not just evil, but deliberate evil.

— And why is the tree called not just the tree of knowledge of evil, but the tree of knowledge of *good* and evil?

— Because the first people would have known good if they had resisted temptation and stayed true to God, stayed with Him. They would have felt a victory over evil and thus would have known good.

The mysteries of books

To be read is a joy for every book. Books love to feel the warmth of our hands and the thoughtfulness of our eyes on their pages.

The books often have to wait for a long time standing on a shelf before people's souls would perceive their contents.

So the books tell each other what is written in them. And when all the stories are told they set each other riddles about their hidden meaning.

A-musing!

(the hidden meaning of a fairy-tale)

— And what is the hidden meaning? Is there one in every book?

— Well, there are no mysteries in a telephone book. And in the fairy-tale "The Wild Swans" by Hans Christian Andersen...

— But I know that tale by heart, the whole of it! There are no mysteries for me in it.

— Sure, you remember everything about the eleven brothers and their sister Eliza. You remember that they were the King's children. So, what does that mean?

— That they were princes and a princess and they were the successors to their father's throne obviously.

— Now think: besides our parents on earth, all of us, people, have got everyone's great Father, and He is... can you guess, who He is?

— It's God. He is called the Heavenly King. He is a King... Wow! That means that all of us are King's children, we are princes and princesses.

— That's right! And that means, that our heritage is the Eternal Life, Paradise, Kingdom of Heaven. It's not a Kingdom in the blue sky that we see, but in the much more beautiful — invisible, spiritual Heaven.

And the Andersen's story is not just about the children of a fairy-tale King, but also about you and me, about all people in the world. So the secret meaning begins to uncover.

— Great! Let me compare more things in it. There is also a stepmother who envies the children and wants to steal the Kingdom from them. She makes the children unrecognizable for their father... Oh, I see! The devil envies us, people much more than the stepmother envies the children, for our future Kingdom is better. And the devil tries to prevent us from coming into this Kingdom of Heaven. Actually, it's quite fascinating, to solve the fairy-tale like a big riddle.

— And we've only started! There are a lot of analogies in that fairy-tale. Here's one more:

the stepmother hid the likeness of children and their Father, she locked them in the birds' bodies and stained Eliza with ugly dark ointment.

— What is the analogy here?

— It's also obvious. There is the image of God in us, the one that is reflected in us like the sun in the dewdrops, and the devil had taught people to let evil into their souls. Evil is like black cover, like dark ointment, like a cloud obscures the God's image in us.

— And the brothers had to be saved, and we should be as well.

— And you surely can't forget that Eliza saved her brothers by making a sacrifice.

— I remember that! I do! She burnt her hands with nettle, and went to the cemetery at night, and she kept silence though she was slandered. And she even mounted the bonfire, although she was not guilty of anything. Oh! Again, it all fits! For how much did Christ the Son of God endure to save us. He was executed in the most horrible way.

— And Eliza putting the shirts on her brothers and freeing them is like the Savior freeing us by his Resurrection. But what we should think about is what would have happened if the brothers hadn't flown up to her to let her put the shirts on them?

— Well, they would have stayed enchanted.

— So we also should accept what Christ has done for us.

— How do we do that?

— By believing that all that is said in the New Testament about Christ our Savior is true. By accepting the sacraments of baptism, penance and communion.

A story about a mole

Once upon a time there lived a mole. His name was Blindy. He was a rich mole. He had a lot of earth. The mole dug long black tunnels in the earth. Not a single ray of light came through those tunnels and there were no other colours in his holes but black. And he wouldn't have seen any other colour anyway, for he was blind. That's why he was called Blindy.

Everything that got in his way in the tunnels became the moles prey. He devoured bugs, worms, larvae, he crunched roots. Blindy was sure that life is completely known and clear to him. The whole world was either earth that could be dug or things that could be eaten — that's what he was sure of. And he had no doubt that everything that existed in the world was black.

One day the mole was digging so close to the surface that he heard quiet knocks; those were two birds picking seeds, sprinkled over the ground.

Blindy overheard them talking.

— How beautiful the day is after the rain had fallen, — twittered one of the birds. — Everything is so clean, the air is so fresh, there are raindrops on the leaves and the sun is sparkling in them, so that the leaves are not just green — they look as if they were glazed.

— And it's going to be even better, — twittered the other bird. The sun will dry all the raindrops, the flowers will spread their petals, sunlight will run through the leaves on the trees and the sky will turn bright blue. And I will fly high, high to the sky and I will bathe in that sweet air in the joyful blue, in the warm light.

Blindy even forgot that he was giving away his listening.

— Hey, you two, what are you lying there? — he shouted from underneath the ground. — What sun are you talking about? I've been digging and digging here for quite a while, and my nose has never ever touched any sun! Your sun is a lie and nothing more! And you've also made up some silly flowers! And the sky! There is no such thing as the sky!

— Who is this? Who is it talking? — the birds were startled. — Oh, poor creature! He's sitting down there and he's never seen the sky. The sky! It's so wonderful! It's so blue! He must see the sky!

— What does that mean — blue? — snorted the mole. — Care to explain what does blue mean?

But whatever the birds sang to the mole, he just snorted: "There is nothing but earth, blackness, roots and worms".

Then the mole went away somewhere down his tunnels and the birds were very upset.

One of the birds was so sorry for the mole. And as the mole couldn't leave his dark world, the bird herself decided to go down to the stuffy black dungeons, and she left her beloved world for the mole's world.

But the mole couldn't get to know the world of light not only because of his dark dungeon. Even more he was stopped by his blindness — physical and spiritual.

To free the mole of all that prevented him from seeing the light the bird decided to take his moleness on herself.

And the bird turned into a mole. And as soon as all mole's features went into the bird, the mole became free of what had kept him in the darkness. He flew from under the ground as a beautiful bird breathed in the air and freedom, opened his eyes to greet the light.

And what happened to the bird? Being a mole in the mole's world hurt her so much that the bird died from that pain. But it was only the mole's body that died, and the bird that had gone down into the dark world, rose again — as a bird and not as a mole.

A-musing!

(How did the Son of God save us)

— But why did the bird go down?! The mole never asked her about it, he didn't even care about the big world. I wish he stayed there, in his black hole. They wanted to give him the best things and he said they were lying.

— That's why the bird pitied him, because the mole rejected the world not because he was mean, but because he was ignorant. The same is when God calls people to enter the eternal life, and they reject paradise, everlasting happiness not because they really don't need them. Like the mole who had known only blackness, people know only material world and can't get through it to God. And what a shame it is that people miss themselves out of the eternal happiness. And they even bridle up, saying there is neither God nor Paradise.

— I think I know what the hidden meaning of the story is! Like the bird went to the underworld so did God, who came to our material world, that ends with death. The bird took away from the mole all that prevented him from seeing the world of light. And Christ, the Son of God took away all our sins that don't let us enter paradise.

— That's true... and the bird was killed by the bad things she took from the mole. And Christ had died on the cross. And in both cases death destroys the things that hold them back. And so the Resurrection happens.

"He took up our pain and bore our suffering, yet we considered him punished by God, stricken by him, and afflicted. But he was pierced for our transgressions, he was crushed for our iniquities; the punishment that brought us peace was on him, and by his wounds we are healed. We all, like sheep, have gone astray, each of us has turned to our own way; and the Lord has laid on him the iniquity of us all. He was oppressed and afflicted, yet he did not open his mouth; he was led like a lamb to the slaughter, and as a sheep before its shearers is silent, so he did not open his mouth. By oppression and judgment he was taken away. Yet who of his generation protested? For he was cut off from the land of the living; for the transgression of my people he was punished". (Isaiah 53:4–8 (New International Version))

A story about an ant

Once upon a time there lived an ant called Grippy Chela. He loved his ant hill under a tall pine tree very much, he knew all the tunnels and halls of it, and ants' paths near his home. But he had never climbed the pine tree yet. The ant had a dream: to see the whole wide world. One day an old ant told Grippy Chela:

— Look at the trunk of our pine. Its bark is wrinkled so that it forms a ladder.

— And can I see the whole world from such ladder? — asked Grippy Chela.

— I don't know, I've never managed to climb that far, — answered the old ant. — The only thing I know is that the higher you climb the more you can see.

— Well, I'm sure to get to the step from which I'll *see everything*.

So the next day he climbed up.

There came the first step.

— There it is — the world! It's a whole forest of grass around our ant hill!

After climbing some more steps he exclaimed:

— No, it looks like the world is not just our ant hill and our pine. The world turns out to consist of two pines and two ant hills. And there is a forest of grass around them.

Every step took his breath away, because he thought, that at last he knew the world, but with every next step the world turned out to be greater. And his previous knowledge appeared to be false.

Grippy Chela didn't regret about those steps that lay beneath, for each of them had brought him a great discovery and gave a new joy. And from the top of the pine tree the ant saw vast forests and the blue sky with hovering birds.

— There it is — the world! But those birds there, they must *see* something even greater and more beautiful. And a plane can rise even higher than the birds can… And someone else can rise higher than that. That means — there is no such highest point which you can *see* the whole world from.

A-musing!

(How a man gets closer to God)

— How interesting! I feel like I've already experienced something like that. What can that be?

— Well, let me tell you what I remember about you when you were a little boy. And you decide if it reminds you of what happened to the little ant.

You were less than a year yet, I held you in my arms pacing around the room, touching different objects and saying their names: "table", "bed", "book", "flowers". That's how I taught you to speak. And I wanted to say the word "God". But what could I have pointed at?

— So what did you do?

— I pointed at the icon and said "God".

— But then I could have thought that God is a wooden plaque with a face drawn on it.

— First of all, icons aren't drawn, they are painted. And the faces on them are called images. And also, showing you the icon, I already knew back then, that afterwards I'll tell you that God is not an icon. Icon is only an image of God, a portrayal. And God Himself is alive and He has created the whole world.

— And did not remember to tell it me afterwards?

— Of course I did. As soon as you began to talk.

— And I don't remember that already. But I must have been very surprised. I must have imagined God being a man who's sitting somewhere in the sky.

— And it's really like the ant's journey. He also left what he had learnt on the lower step, and climbed the next one to learn more about the world and then to leave that step behind as well...

— And then I already can remember myself which invisible steps I took to get closer to God. Then I knew that God was not a person, but a Spirit. But I thought that Spirit means air, but you've told me I was wrong.

And that's true: as soon as I learn something, as soon as I mount this step — I need to leave it and climb up the next one. You've also read to me that "God is Love" (I st Epistle of John 4:8(American standart)), but at the same time you've told me that it's not like a man who feels love, it's Love without a body. That means God is immaterial.

— Right, and a man who's created after the image and likeness of God resembles Him not because he has a body — actually, this is the difference.

— And when we were reading the "A-musing", every story was like a step; every step surprised me. I was surprised that God can be in all places at one moment and that He can be in all times. And that God can say "Me" about Himself, but we have no such word that could explain everything about who He is. I was surprised that the One who can name Himself "Me" has always existed, and there had been no one before him. And he named the things that He wanted to create and they appeared and became His material Words, and there was life in everything.

— And do you remember me telling you that the Beginning of everything, the Word and Life of all creations are united? The three of them together are one. And God is the Holy Trinity. Thee Father, the Son and the Holy Spirit.

— You know, I like mounting this invisible ladder not only because it leads closer and closer to God. Something special is happening to my soul: it seems to resemble a cup, and the cup is growing bigger and deeper and is filling with wonderful light.

— In ancient times there was a saint Afanasi the Great. He said that we can't know who God is. We can only say that He is neither this nor that.

— Wait, but we say the same about our inner "self" that is hidden in the very centre of the soul. We also say about it that it is not our body, it is neither our feelings nor our thoughts, but someone who sees and names them from the inside.

— See, how it all matches! Rising towards God, whom we seek in the world is similar to meeting the Image of God that we find in ourselves. Both journeys are made by refusing the things that are not God.

You can't behold God, that's why there is no end of this ascension. You can unveils and discover Him for yourself more and more. So you can go from joy to even greater joy.

Printed in the United States
By Bookmasters